A GROUNDWOOD BOOK

DOUGLAS & McINTYRE

TORONTO VANCOUVER BERKELEY

Inanna

FROM THE MYTHS OF ANCIENT SUMER

KIM ECHLIN

ILLUSTRATED BY

LINDA WOLFSGRUBER

ACKNOWLEDGEMENTS

I would like to thank Dr. Douglas Frayne at the University of Toronto for his guidance while I was working on these translations. His knowledge, unbounded generosity and deep love of scholarship are a continuing inspiration. The Electronic Text Corpus of Sumerian Literature from Oxford University publishes the most recent translations of new texts and makes them available to anyone with access to a computer. I am also very grateful to W.S. Merwin for reading and commenting on early versions of this poem.

Groundwood Books / Douglas & McIntyre
720 Bathurst Street, Suite 500, Toronto, Ontario
Distributed in the USA by Publishers Group West
1700 Fourth Street, Berkeley, CA 94710

We acknowledge for their financial support of our publishing program the Canada Council for the Arts, the Government of Canada through the Book Publishing Industry Development Program (BPIDP), the Ontario Arts Council and the Government of Ontario through the Ontario Media Development Corporation's Ontario Book Initiative.

ONTARIO ARTS COUNCIL
CONSEIL DES ARTS DE L'ONTARIO

National Library of Canada Cataloging in Publication
Echlin, Kim A.
Inanna: from the myths of ancient Sumer / by Kim Echlin;
illustrated by Linda Wolfsgruber.
Poems.
ISBN 0-88899-496-6
1. Inanna (Sumerian deity) – Poetry. I. Wolfsgruber, Linda II. Title.
PS8559.C48I53 2003   C811'.54   C2002-906143-1
PZ7

Library of Congress Control Number: 2002117069

Design by Michael Solomon
Printed and bound in China by Everbest Printing Company Ltd.

For Patsy Aldana
K E & LW

TABLE OF CONTENTS

Inanna's Family Tree

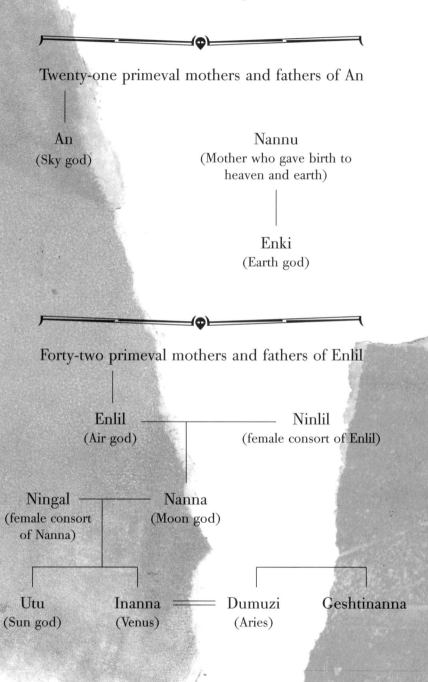

Twenty-one primeval mothers and fathers of An

An
(Sky god)

Nannu
(Mother who gave birth to
heaven and earth)

Enki
(Earth god)

Forty-two primeval mothers and fathers of Enlil

Enlil
(Air god)

Ninlil
(female consort of Enlil)

Ningal
(female consort
of Nanna)

Nanna
(Moon god)

Utu
(Sun god)

Inanna
(Venus)

Dumuzi
(Aries)

Geshtinanna

ABOUT THIS TRANSLATION

The stories of Inanna come from Sumer, an ancient land tucked between the Tigris and Euphrates Rivers in what is now Iraq. Inanna's great myths and hymns were told and sung four thousand years ago — long before the stories of the Bible and the Koran, before the myths of the Greeks and Romans.

Inanna was the daughter of the moon couple, Nanna and Ningal, and a great-granddaughter of An (heaven) and Nannu (mother of heaven and earth). The people of Sumer believed that she was directly descended from the ancient fathers and mothers who appeared when the first mountain was born out of the primordial sea.

The Sumerians were fascinated by the stars and they speculated on the meaning of the stars' movements across the night sky. They thought of Inanna when they looked at the planet Venus, which shines with the first light in the evening and the first light at dawn. They used to pray:

> Great light, you are the one of all divine power
> and no god can compete with you...
> You go from moonlight to star,
> you go from star to moonlight.

The stories I have included trace the path of Inanna's growth from her youth to her maturity. As a young girl, she showed the first signs of her determined will by caring for a tree from which she wanted to carve her sacred throne and bed. When she grew older and braver and more beautiful, she visited Enki, the god of earth and wisdom. In a drinking contest, she won the powers of civilization from him. After that, she fell in love with the shepherd Dumuzi. Their love story is one of the most beautiful ever told.

But Inanna wanted power beyond heaven and earth, power beyond making her lover a king. From her suffering in the underworld she gained new powers and she was able to return to earth with new strength. She now knew how to defend herself and she could be ferocious. When she was angry she filled the wells of the land with blood and destroyed the mountains. She knew how to create and to destroy and to name things. The people began to worship her.

It is believed that Inanna was widely worshipped for several thousand years. There are dozens of great hymns to her written by the Sumerian priestess Enheduanna, who may have been the world's first poet and who wrote in the first system of writing called cuneiform. These symbols look like small wedges or slender triangles. Enheduanna, one of the few female scribes, would have written by pressing her words into damp clay tablets with a sharp stylus and baking them dry.

Inanna's stories were not originally written down as a single narrative but I have arranged the myths chronologically. In Sumerian storytelling, confrontations between the gods are vigorous, strong and direct. The love stories are unembarrassed and sexually explicit. All the myths combine reverence and awe and exuberant joy, as if new energies were being recognized and celebrated. I have tried to keep as much of this as I could. To make the Sumerian style more accessible to our contemporary ears, I have compressed many of the original repetitions and have explained some of the names and cultural ideas in the poems.

I discovered Inanna when I was looking for myths to tell to my own two daughters, Olivia and Sara. As soon as I read Inanna's stories I loved them. Though she is four thousand years old, she is still full of the kind of energy that makes the world new. She is fearless and strong and resourceful and creative. The translations I found were mostly for scholars and I wanted to create something that any willing reader could enjoy. And so I collected all the fragments I could find about Inanna and reworked them as a single story for this book.

My daughters have always liked stories about adventurous characters who come up with amazing solutions to tricky situations. One of them likes marriages in her stories and the other likes battles. Inanna's stories are full of all these things. As I worked at adapting them for this translation, I was impressed at the range of narratives in the Inanna collection. She can do anything and she is not afraid to try.

As I think of Inanna, and the first poets who wrote hymns to her, I cannot help but wonder how her stories sounded to the people of Sumer. These translations are an echo of a language and a people that have been lost for a very long time. But Inanna's power and beauty shine through like the reflected light of the moon.

Kim Echlin
Toronto, 2003

Inanna

THE BEGINNING

IN the first days and nights and years
everything was brought into being.
Bread was baked in the shrines
and names were put in their places.

The god An carried away heaven.
The god Enlil carried away earth.
The realms were separate from then on.

The underworld was given to Ereshkigal.
Enki who played tricks tried to sail to that dark place.
Stones made of wind and stones made of ice
   beat him back.
Waves like wolves swallowed the bow of his boat
   in their teeth.
Waves like lions caught the stern in their claws.

The realms are separate to this day.

13

INANNA

IN those first days and nights
the huluppu tree took root on the banks
of the river Euphrates.
A young woman saw it and she loved it.

In time she would be great.
She would wear the heavens on her head like a crown
and the earth on her feet like fine sandals.
Mountains would bow low to her.
She would dare to go down to the dark underworld
and find her way back.

She would have great power.
Only she would be able to make man into woman
and woman into man.
Only she would destroy what should not be destroyed
and create what should not be created.

But when that little huluppu tree first grew
she had no power.
Her destiny was a small shoot reaching up.

Her name was Inanna.

THE HULUPPU TREE

THERE was a wild storm.
   The whirling south wind ripped out the huluppu tree
by its roots and tossed it into the river.

Inanna rescued it from the waters
and planted it in her garden.
She wanted to carve her shining throne and her bed
from its trunk.

Time passed.
Five years,
Ten years.
The tree grew tall
   and thick.

A snake made a nest
   in its roots.
A bird raised its young
   among the branches.
A stranger called Lilith
   lived in its trunk.

Inanna flew into a rage!
She had tended this tree in her own garden.
She had been patient and waited.
She would not let someone else make it their home.
The tree belonged to her.

Inanna raged and wept
but she could not get the snake and
   the bird and Lilith to go away.

She asked her brother Utu for help.
She said,
"I took care of my tree and waited.
Get them out of my tree."
But the Sun god would do nothing.

Inanna went weeping to her
    brother Gilgamesh,
the hero who was
    two-thirds god and one-third man.
She said,
"Help me get my tree back."

17

Gilgamesh put on his battle armor
and strode into Inanna's garden.
He lifted his bronze ax high
and swung it down with all his force
on the snake in the roots.
Inanna's tree shuddered.
That single blow bent and battered the branches
and cracked the thick trunk.

The bird flew with its young into the mountains.
Lilith smashed up her home and fled in terror
to a place where there was no one.

Then Gilgamesh carved a shining throne and bed
from the trunk for Inanna.
And Inanna wove a headpiece and mantle
from the branches and roots for Gilgamesh.

Inanna took care of her tree.
She defied great Utu to defend her tree.
Her destiny was great!

THE DRINKING MATCH

INANNA crowned herself!
She wanted to make the whole world,
shepherd to sheepfold,
as radiant and beautiful,
as perfect and luminous as she was.
She wanted everyone to look up
and know that she was the evening star.
She wanted the whole world lighted up
with the pure light of the star
that shines before night's darkness
and before the break of dawn.

She was delighted with her breasts
and her vulva.
She was exuberant and she loved herself.
She was young and delighted
with everything.
Heaven and earth could not contain her delight.

Inanna said,
"I am Queen of Heaven.
I shall visit Enki.
I shall go to the deep sweet waters
of the sacred river Abzu
and honor great Enki."

She set out alone for the river
where fresh water mixes with salt.

Now, Enki knows all things,
even the hearts of the gods.

He called to his servant Isimud.
"Inanna is coming to my temple.
Give her butter cake to eat.
Pour cold water to refresh her.
Offer her beer before the statue of the lion.
Invite her to my table
and treat her as my equal."

So Inanna was welcomed into the temple
and after a while Enki came to toast her.
He drank beer with her.
They drank and drank some more.
They drank from the cups of Urash
Mother of the earth.

Enki, God of Wisdom,
toasted Inanna.
"In the name of my power,
in the name of my holy shrine
I give you
priesthood!
The crown!
The throne!"

20

Inanna said, "I take them."

Enki raised his glass to Inanna again.
"I give you
travel and home,
loosened hair and bound hair,
dark and light garments."

Inanna said, "I take them."

They drank and drank and drunk
Enki kept toasting Inanna and giving away things.
"I give you the art of love-making.
I give you all kinds of speech
straight and slanderous,
praising and adoring.

"I give you the art of the hero,
the art of power,
the art of treachery
and of honesty.
I give you rejoicing and lamentation.

"I give you the crafts,
the wood-worker and the copper-worker,
the scribe and the smith,
the leather-maker and the fuller,
the builder and reed-worker.

"I give you
the kindling of fire,
the quenching of fire,
the kindling of strife,
the quenching of strife."

Inanna said, "I take them."

Until then only the gods possessed
the powers of civilization.
They were called
   the holy *me*.

The beer made
   Enki munificent.
He could not resist Inanna's beauty.

With the drink in him Enki kept raising his cup.
"I give you descent to the underworld,
ascent from the underworld.
I give you Truth."

He was swaying under his own generosity.
The last gift he gave to Inanna
was the art of making decisions.

There are no greater gifts
than the powers of civilization
and Inanna did not hesitate for a moment.
She took hold of everything.

Finally Enki fell over.
Inanna decided to sail away
with her gifts on the Boat of Heaven.

When Enki woke up
he could not remember anything.
His head throbbed.

Things were missing.
He had been robbed.

Enki could not remember
    anything at all.
He called to Isimud,
"Where is the priesthood?
Where are the crown and the throne,
the art of the hero, and power and treachery?
Where are rejoicing and lamentation?
Where is honesty?"

Isimud answered, "My king gave them to Inanna."

Enki rubbed his head.
"Did I give away love-making?
Did I give away the art of making decisions?"

Isimud said, "My king gave them all to Inanna."

Enki said, "Where is the Boat of Heaven?"

Isimud answered, "Inanna sailed away on it."

Then Enki commanded, "Go!
Take my guards and bring it back!"

So they chased the Boat of Heaven.
Isimud called out, "Inanna! Enki has sent me.
Hear his sacred word."

Inanna turned and called back, "What does he want?"

"Enki says that you may go on your way
but you are to send back
the holy gifts in the Boat of Heaven."

Inanna said, "What is that?
He gave me these gifts.
He toasted me and gave me everything
in the name of his holy temple.
Is this his sacred word!
All lies?"

Before she could finish
Isimud laid hands on the Boat of Heaven.
But Inanna called for her servant Ninshubar
and together they took back the boat.

Enki sent fifty giants.
Enki sent fifty sea monsters.
But nothing could stop Inanna.
Nothing could swallow the bow
or claw over the stern of the Boat of Heaven.

When Inanna arrived in her own city at the Gate of Joy
the people rejoiced.
They slaughtered bulls and sacrificed sheep.
They poured beer.
They were in awe of Inanna.
The holy gifts were unloaded and given to the people.

Then something strange happened.
There were gifts that Enki had not given.
Things appeared that were not in his temple
in the deep sweet waters of the sacred river Abzu.
Things that Enki did not give away.
New things.

The new gifts were the art of being woman.
They were women's songs
and drums and stringed instruments
and the perfection of all the holy gifts.

Inanna gave everything to her people
and she named the place
the Lapis Lazuli Quay.

It was not long before Enki came visiting.
He said to Inanna,
"In the name of my power
in the name of my holy shrine
the gifts I gave you
shall remain in your holy temple.
Your people will prosper and be my allies
and their children will sing your praise."

Inanna's great destiny
shone over her people.
They sang her radiance.
They sang her beauty and her song.

SONGS OF LOVE

INANNA wandered in the darkness.
She was radiant and lovely.
Was she in love?

Sometimes she saw
   the shepherd
   and she thought
   she was in love.
Sometimes she saw
   the farmer
   and she thought
   she was in love.
Which did
   she love?

Love's First Song

UTU spoke tenderly to his daughter.
Utu the Sun god sang to Inanna,

The flax in the garden is lovely
The flax is lovely and ripe
You need a length of flax cloth
I will dig the flax for you.

Inanna answered,

Who will ret the flax for me?
Who will ret the flax?

I will bring it to you
all retted.

Who will spin the flax for me?
Who will spin the flax?

I will bring it to you
all spun.

Who will twine
the flax for me?
Who will twine the flax?

I will bring it to you
all twined.

Who will warp the flax for me?
Who will warp the flax?

I will bring it to you
all warped.

Who will weave the flax for me?
Who will weave the flax?

I will bring it to you
all woven.

Who will bleach the flax for me?
Who will bleach the flax?

I will bring it to you
all bleached.

Who will lie down on the flax with me?
Who will lie down on the flax linen?

You will lie down on it with
    the shepherd.
You will lie down on the flax linen
    with Dumuzi.

Then Inanna answered,
Dumuzi will be the man of
    my heart.
He speaks to my heart.
His sheep are thick with wool.
The shepherd will be my love.

29

Lie in the Moonlight

WHAT love does not begin
at first sight?
Inanna was with her friends in the square.
She danced and sang all day.
At dusk Dumuzi saw her.
He came toward her.

Inanna said, "He had beautiful eyes.
He tried to take my hand.
He tried to kiss me.
I told him, 'Wild bull,
   let me go.
I have to go home.
How will I explain to my mother
that I stayed out with you?'
He had beautiful eyes."

30

And Dumuzi said, "Let me teach you the lies of women.
Tell your mother you were out with your girlfriend.
Tell her you played the tambourine and the flute
and sang songs in the square.
Tell her you danced with your girlfriend
the whole night.
Come with me.
Let me make love with you in the moonlight."

Inanna sighed, "I wanted to go with him.
but I also wanted to please my mother."

31

Courting Outside the Door

DUMUZI called at Inanna's door,
"What are you doing?"

Inanna and her women called back,
"I am washing with soap from the white stone bowl.
I am softening my skin with sweet oil.
I am darkening my eyes with kohl.
I am combing my hair loose and long.
I am slipping gold bracelets around my wrists
and blue lapis beads around my neck."

Dumuzi called again,
"Let me see. Let me come in.
I will give you fine gifts.
I will bring you whatever you want.
Your eyes are lovely.
You are your mother's honey.
Your lips are honey."

Heaven and earth were not wide enough.
Inanna shone with first love.
She danced and sang.
She said to her women,
"When Dumuzi comes
    let the musicians play.
I will pour wine for him.
I will please his heart."

The women behind the door called out,
"How will Dumuzi give?
Is his sheepfold full? Is he generous?
Will he give lambs as well as ewes?"

Dumuzi called back,
"I will bring lambs to the house."

The women inside said,
"Will he bring kids as well as goats?"

Dumuzi called back,
"I will bring kids with me to the house."

The women insisted,
"Will the lambs be as fine as the ewes?"

Dumuzi answered,
"I will bring all that you want."

Then the women laughed and teased,
"Our nipples grow firm, our smooth skin has hair!"

Inanna joined the song,

        "Dance! Dance!
        Sprinkle sweet-smelling water in the room.
        I am beautiful
        I will please him
        I will please Dumuzi."

Changeable Heart

Utu wanted Inanna to marry Dumuzi.
The Sun god praised the shepherd.
He took her to see the full sheepfold.
But Inanna turned away.

She said, "I am the star of my mother's womb.
I will not marry the shepherd.
I will never be his wife."

"Why?" said great Utu. "Why?
His milk is good, his butter is good,
his work is fine.
Why do you change your mind?"

Inanna said, "I like the farmer better.
He will bring me flax for cloth
and barley for beer.
He will bring me fresh lettuce to eat.
I will not marry the shepherd.
I like the farmer better."

When Dumuzi heard what was going on
he went straight to the farmer and shouted,
"Come out! Show that you are better than I am.

Show me your black cloth! I will show you my black ewe.
Pour me your beer! I will pour you my churned milk.
Lay out your bread and your beans.
I will feed you my sweet curds and fine cheese."

Then Dumuzi strode back to the steppe,
taunting the farmer as he walked.

The farmer followed him and called out,
"Shepherd, bring your sheep to my land.
They can graze in my grain fields
and drink from my canals.
I do not want to fight with you."

"Good then," said Dumuzi.
"We will be friends, farmer.
You will even come to my wedding."

37

Dumuzi strode back to Inanna.
She said again, "I will not marry you.
I am the star of my mother's womb.
Without my mother, you are nothing but a wanderer.
Without my father, you are nothing but a vagrant.
Without my brother, you are a nothing
wandering on the dark paths of the steppe.
I will not marry you!"

Dumuzi answered tenderly, "Why do you want to quarrel?
Let us talk things over.
Come, soft.
My mother is as good as your mother.
Talk it over with me.
My father is as good as your father.
Come, listen.
My sister Geshtinanna is as good as yours.
I am as good as your brother Utu.

Inanna provoked Dumuzi.
He was tender.
She turned from him.
He stayed.
She felt her anger kindled and quenched.
His voice stirred her heart
and her thighs.
He had lovely eyes.
He filled her with desire.

Dumuzi stood in the arch of the lapis door.
Inanna danced and sang.
She sent word to Utu, "Bring me Dumuzi.
I will have the shepherd.
Put flowers and sweet herbs on my bed.
Bring me the man I love.
Put his hand in my hand.
Press his heart next to my heart.
Our pleasure will be sweet.
I will rest my head on his arm.
Our sleep will be sweet."

And then she sang to Dumuzi,

    My love
    Your eyes are beautiful
    Your face is sweet
    Sweet as honey
    Wild bull
    My love.

    Warrior
    You have taken hold of me
    You will possess me
    I come to you trembling
    I will follow you to the honey bed.

You have taken me
my love
I come freely to you
You march on me
and conquer me on the honey bed.

My love
I will do sweet things to you
I will give you honey
in our bed dripping with honey
Bridegroom
You love me
Speak to my mother, I give myself to you
Speak to my father, he shall offer you gifts.

You my love
you love me
I cannot wait
    until you do sweet things to me
Your body is sweet as honey
I cannot wait
    until you rouse yourself for me
Put your hand on it for me
I give myself to you.

INANNA and her mother and her women
made the house ready.
They sent word to the shepherd and the farmer,
    to the fowler and the fisherman.

    To the shepherd I send this messenger
    Treat me tenderly with your best butter and milk.

    To the farmer I send this messenger
    Treat me tenderly with your sweetest honey and wine.

    To the fowler I send this messenger
    Treat me tenderly with your plumpest birds.

    To the fisherman with his net in the canebrake
    Treat me tenderly with your fat golden carp.

Dumuzi led the bridesmen to Inanna.
They carried many gifts to the house.
Dumuzi had butter and buttermilk in sacred vessels
    on his shoulder.
He stood outside and called, "Open the door!"

41

Inanna turned to her mother.
She stood and waited.

Inanna's mother sang,

>   Do not be afraid
>   His mother will cherish you as your own mother
>   His father will cherish you as your own father
>   He will be like your own brother and sister
>   He will be like your own father and mother
>   Open the door
>   It is time
>   Open the door.

Inanna washed with soap from the white stone bowl.
She softened her skin with sweet oil.
She put on her royal dress.
She took the royal pin in her hand
and arranged the lapis beads around her neck.
She waited.

Dumuzi pushed open the door.
He came into the house like moonlight.
He gazed at Inanna.
He rejoiced in her
and embraced her
and kissed her.

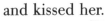

Inanna said, "He enters the house.
Dumuzi is my king.
The shepherd is my king."

Dumuzi answered, "My wife, come with me.
I will bring you to the house of my god.
You will sit in honor before my god.
Your table will be splendid
and only you will eat there.
Not my mother or my sister or my uncle.
You
my wife,
you shall not weave for me
or spin or card or warp for me.
You wear the golden broach pin of the queen.
Inanna
my wife."

44

The wild bull Dumuzi
came into the house like moonlight,
radiance on the horizon,
soft light in the heaven.

The women sang,

Inanna longs for the holy bed
She longs for the heart's bed
Her body stirs and longs
She longs for the bed of the king
and for the bed of the queen.

She waits for her beloved
She waits for her king
She calls the king to the bed
She calls him beloved.

The king goes to her holy thighs
He embraces his queen
They lie hand in hand
They lie heart to heart.

Inanna Sings Her Love

HE lies down beside me on our honey bed
He takes my hand in his hand
He puts his foot by my foot
He takes my lips in his mouth
His love is like a bracelet on my wrist
like gold on my neck
like silver on my arms
like a precious jewel on my buttocks.

He takes me into his garden
I stand with him in the tall trees
I lie down with him in the fallen trees
My precious sweet
The wild bull speaks to me in the apple trees
My precious sweet
The wild bull speaks to me in the fig trees
We make love standing up and lying down
in his garden.

47

Love's Last Song

DUMUZI said, "You are your mother's honey.
Your eyes are lovely.
Your barley beer is good.
Your ale is good.
My sweet honey lips kissing you is good.
For as long as you live keep this oath to me.
Say you will not lie down with another."

Inanna answered, "I will make an oath to you,
you of the beautiful eyes.
You will place your right hand between my legs
and your left hand will cradle my head.
You will take my lips in yours.

"This is the oath of woman
you of the beautiful eyes.
Oh Dumuzi my love you are beautiful."

The women sang,

> Inanna! He laid you down on the honey bed
> You kissed his beautiful eyes
> He made love fifty times and he waited for you
> each time
> you trembled beneath him.
>
> When his hands held your hips
> that time was precious

The days were precious
when the shepherd lay
wrapped in the sweetness of your holy body
Those hours were precious.

And when he was sated he said, "Let me go."
And you said, "You are still a child.
One day the gods will know you as a man.
For now, I let you go."

THE UNDERWORLD

INANNA sailed away on the Boat of Heaven.
She stole the holy powers.
She had truth.
The marriage bed was not wide enough for her.
Heaven and earth were not wide enough for her.
Inanna wanted to go to the underworld.
She wanted the divine power of the underworld.

INANNA put on her traveling hat
and arranged her dark hair.
She put on her lapis beads
and hung two egg-shaped beads on her breasts.
She darkened her eyes with kohl
and put on the traveling vest.
She slipped on her gold ring and took up her royal lapis rod.
She turned away from heaven and earth.
She turned her wisdom to the underworld.

Inanna said to her servant Ninshubar,
"I am going down to the underworld.
If I do not come back after three days
beat a drum for me.
Cut your face with mourning,
cut your eyes and your nose and your ears,
cut your buttocks and dress in mourning rags.
Visit the gods for me.
Ask them to save me.
Sing this lament to them.

Great holy god!
Do not let your Inanna die
Your precious pure gold is alloyed
Your precious lapis is broken
Your precious boxwood is chipped
Do not let Inanna die in the underworld.

She told Ninshubar, "Sing this song first to Enlil.
If Enlil will not help then sing it to Nanna.
If Nanna will not help then sing it to Enki.
Enki once braved the underworld too.
Enki possesses the water of life and the plant of life.
Enki might help."

Then Inanna left and her servant tried to follow.
But the traveler said, "Go back!
Do not forget what I have told you."

INANNA arrived at the door of
the underworld
and banged on it hard.
She shouted at the doorman,
    "Open up, Neti!
I am all alone and I want to come in.
Open up!"

51

Neti asked, "Who are you?"

She answered, "I am Inanna traveling east."

Neti said, "If you are traveling east
why do you come here?
Why do you travel on the road
from which no traveler returns?"

Inanna said,
"Ereshkigal mourns
for Gugalana, her husband.
I have come to his wake."

Neti went back to Ereshkigal and said,
"A girl waits alone outside the door.
She demands to come in.
She says she is Inanna."

Ereshkigal said, "What has she brought?
What is she wearing?"

Neti answered, "She is wearing her traveling hat.
She is wearing lapis beads and eyes darkened
    with kohl.
She is wearing a gold ring
    and carries the royal rod."

Ereshkigal slapped her thigh and bit her lip.
She said, "That is my sister!"
Bolt the seven doors.
If she wishes to come in she leaves something
at each door
until she is naked."

Neti bolted the seven doors and said to Inanna,
"Come in. Give me your hat and enter."
Her hat was taken from her head.

Inanna said, "What is this!"

"Quiet!" said Neti.
"Do not speak against the rites of this place.
Its ways must be fulfilled."

At the second door her lapis beads were removed.

Inanna said, "What is this!"

"Quiet!" said Neti.
"Do not speak against the rites of this place.
Its ways must be fulfilled."

At the third door she gave up her twin egg-shaped beads.
At the fourth door she gave up her traveling vest.
At the fifth door she gave up her gold ring.
At the sixth door she gave up her lapis rod.
At the seventh door she gave up her traveling dress.
Inanna was stripped naked.

Then she passed into the underworld.

Inanna stood naked.
Then she pushed Ereshkigal aside.
Naked, she seated herself down
on the throne of the underworld.

The seven judges of that dark place judged Inanna.
They called her guilty.
They condemned her to death.
They struck her down and they hung her body from a hook.

Inanna was a corpse.

Up above
    after waiting for three days and nights
Ninshubar cut her face with mourning.
She cut her eyes and nose
    and her ears and buttocks
and dressed in mourning rags.

She sang before Enlil,

> Great holy god!
> Do not let your Inanna die
> Your precious pure gold
>   is alloyed
> Your precious lapis
>   is broken
> Your precious boxwood is chipped
> Do not let Inanna die in the underworld.

Enlil was full of rage.
"My daughter had heaven and earth
and now she wants the underworld too.
No one should try to possess
the divine powers of the underworld.
Who would go there
    and expect to come back?"

Ninshubar left him.
She sang before Nanna
but Nanna refused to help.

Then Ninshubar sang
    to Enki who knows all things,
even the hearts of the gods.

Enki said, "What has my daughter done?
I fear for her."

He took a bit of dirt from under his fingernail
and he made some tiny creatures.
He gave them the plant of life and the water of life.
He said to them, "Take this plant and this water
    to the underworld.
Flit through the doors like flies
and slip through the doors like ghosts.
Follow the moans of Ereshkigal.
When you see her you will know her.
Her holy shoulders are naked,
her breasts are shrunken,
her nails are sharp,
her hair is tangled like wild leeks.
Mourn with her, moan and groan with her.
She will offer you a river of water and a field
    of grain
but do not accept any gifts.
She will ask you what you want.
Say to her, 'Give us that dead body
    on the hook.'
She will say it is worthless
    and you will ask again.
Then sprinkle it with this water
    and these plants."

Enki's creatures flitted and slipped
    through the underworld
toward the moans of Ereshkigal.
They groaned with her, "Oh my heart,
    my aching heart."

57

She said, "Creatures, what do you want?"
They pointed to Inanna.
Ereshkigal said, "That is nothing."
They said, "That is what we want.
Give us that dead body on the hook."

Ereshkigal gave them Inanna's body.
They sprinkled it with the water of life
and the plant of life.

Inanna came back to life.

S H E was trying to leave the underworld
when the seven judges took hold of her.
They are called the Anuna
and they are fearsome.
They have never tasted food or drink.
They accept no gifts.
They have never felt a lover's embrace
or a child's kiss.
They wrench wife from husband
and they tear father from child.

The Anuna surrounded Inanna like a reed fence
and they imprisoned her
and they rose with her.
They said, "If you want to go back
you must give us someone in your place."

Up above,
Ninshubar saw Inanna
    and she threw herself down.
The Anuna said, "We will take her."

Inanna said, "Ninshubar mourned for me.
She sang for me and brought me back to life.
How could I ever turn her over to you?
Go on."

59

They saw Inanna's singer sitting in the dust.
He was dressed in mourning rags.
The judges said, "We will take him."

But Inanna said, "He cut himself for me.
How could I ever turn him over to you?"

They saw Inanna's mother and her son
and they saw Inanna's women
sitting in the dust wearing filthy mourning rags.
Each time the Anuna said, "We will take this one."
Each time Inanna said, "No! They are mourning for me."

Then they saw Dumuzi dressed like a king
sitting on his throne under the great apple tree on the plain.

Inanna said to him, "How much longer
would you have sat there dressed like a king
while I was in the underworld?"

She judged Dumuzi.
She found him guilty.
She said to the Anuna, "Take him!"
They laid hold of Dumuzi.
They poured the milk from his churns
and they took away his flute
so he could not play for Inanna.

61

DUMUZI wailed and turned pale.
He cried out to Utu, "I am your brother.
I brought butter to your mother's house.
Turn my hands into snakes' hands
and my feet into snakes' feet.
Let me get away!"

Utu could not bear to see Dumuzi's tears.
He turned the shepherd's hands and feet
into snakes
and the king slipped away.

Inanna wept.
She had to find her husband.
She tore at her hair like esparto grass
and she cried out,
"Wives in your husbands' arms,
where is my husband?
Children in your fathers' arms,
where is my child?
Where is Dumuzi?"

A fly buzzed in holy Inanna's ear.
It said, "If I show you where he is,
what will you give me?"

Inanna said, "I will give you what you want.
I will give you life in the beer-house,
on the windows and on the walls.
You will hear everything men say."

63

So a swarm of flies chased down Dumuzi
where he tried to hide on the steppe.
Who can hide from flies?
Inanna handed over her husband to the seven judges
and he was terrified.
But his sister Geshtinanna came looking for him.
She loved him.
The sister wept for her brother.

She approached Inanna.
She said, "Holy goddess, my brother is afraid.
Take me in his place.
I will go in his place to the underworld."

This was love.
This was compassion.

Inanna was moved.
She said to Dumuzi who wept, "Your sister is willing to help you.
You will go to the underworld for half the year
and she will take your place for half the year.
Someone must stay when someone returns
from the place of death."

Inanna had heaven and earth
and she wanted more.
She wanted the divine
powers of the
underworld.
Inanna came back
from death
and she sent
her lover
in her place.

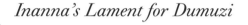

Inanna's Lament for Dumuzi

I MISS you Dumuzi
I miss you
I weep for you
My love, I weep for you
I mourn in the mountains
I mourn in the cities
I mourn in the deserts and plains
Oh my love
I miss you.

She wept.
She was Dumuzi's equal.
Inanna wept.
Her husband was no more.

Inanna mourned
and wept.
Her lover was no more.

65

DESTROYER

INANNA was now a fierce warrior.
She walked through heaven and over earth.
Mount Ebih would not bow down to her.

The god Enlil said, "You cannot conquer the mountain."
Inanna said, "Ebih does not bow down in respect.
I will fill the soaring mountain with terror.
Let my holy games begin!"

She called up a great storm.
She stirred up a raging wind.
Rocks crashed down the mountainside.
Snakes spat venom from gaping cracks.
She set fire to the thick forests
and she killed
    the oak trees with drought.
She made blood run
    through the rivers.
The deer and small creatures
    tried to run away and were lost.
Inanna roared
    like thunder.
She was drenched
    with blood.
She made Ebih bend
    its nose to the dust.

66

She sang,

> I am the milk of the gods
> The mountains are in my hands
>   and at my feet
> I am the guts of the battle
> All will look to me with awe.

67

A New Song

INANNA was tired and lay down and slept.
The shepherd Shukaletuda came upon her.
He raped her and ran away.
Inanna woke up in a rage
and she filled the wells of the land with blood.
Blood flowed through the canals into the orchards.

Slaves found nothing to drink but blood.
No one knew when Inanna's terror would end.
She said, "I will search the caves and steppe
for the one who did this to me."
She said to Enki, "I will not stop until you give me that man."

At last Enki gave him to her.
Then Inanna stretched herself across the sky
like a rainbow and touched the earth.
Shukaletuda was terrified and tried to hide again.

Inanna found him in the mountains.
"Dog! Pig!" she said. "How could you!"
He said, "Storm winds blew mountain dust into my eyes.
I could not get it out.
I thought you were a ghost lying below a shady tree.
I did not know it was you."

Inanna said, "You shall die! You are nothing to me!
But your name shall not be forgotten.
Your name will make the songs sweet.
Shepherds will sing these songs as they churn their butter.
Singers will sing these songs in the palace."

A Praise Song

INANNA sang,

I conquer the mountains
I heap up human heads
like dust
I sow heads like seed.

I am a woman
and a laughing young man
I am a perfect woman
I am a prostitute
I am a man's friend
I am a woman's friend
I am queen
My light shines
through everything
Before me
all things are filled with awe.

CREATOR

INANNA saw men taunting a lonely girl
in the market square.
She saw a mother who held a child
look down on the girl from a window.
Inanna wanted to change this.
She embraced the young girl's fierceness.
She prayed over the girl.
She said, "This girl will have power."
She broke the silver broach pin
that holds a woman's robe.
She blessed this girl's heart as a man's.
She gave her a man's mace.
This new woman was dear to Inanna.
She named her Reed-marsh woman.
Then Inanna saw a man and she broke
   his mace.
She pinned the silver broach pin on him.
She told him to join the woman.
She named him Reed-marsh man.
Inanna created a new man and a new woman.
She put new names in place.
Inanna shines over her people.
They sing her radiance.
They sing her beauty and her song.

GLOSSARY

An: Sky (Heaven) god. An and Ki were father and mother of all the gods. An's other names are: King of Heaven and Earth, King of All the Lands.

Enki: Earth god. Also associated with water and wisdom. Enki is often credited with the creation of the earth and of humans. In some stories, Enki creates the waters by filling the mighty Euphrates with his sperm. In the story, "Enki and the World Order," Enki assigns the gods their powers. It is in this story that Inanna is told by Enki, "You destroy what should not be destroyed; you create what should not be created."

Enlil: Air god, sometimes called Great Mountain.

Ereshkigal: Goddess of the underworld, death goddess, sister of Inanna.

Geshtinanna: Sister of Dumuzi. She is also represented as a divine figure, a dream interpreter, a singer.

Gilgamesh: Brother of Inanna, the hero of an epic poem in which he bravely quests for the plant of immortality and loses it to a snake.

Gugalana: Husband of Ereshkigal, Great Bull of Heaven.

huluppu tree: The sacred tree of Inanna, believed now to be a type of willow.

lapis lazuli: A semi-precious hard opaque stone ranging in color from pale blue to royal blue and indigo. It was a sign of royalty, used to carve sacred objects and found in temples and royal tombs.

me (pronounced MAY): Powers specific to Sumerian culture. Their possession implies both absolute power and absolute responsibility for their implementation in the world. When Inanna steals the holy *me* from Enki and adds some new ones herself, she is establishing her enormous and wide-ranging power. *Me* is believed to be derived from the Sumerian verb "to be."

Nanna: Moon god, father of Inanna.

Utu: Sun god, brother of Inanna. In the story of Enki and the world order, Utu is called father of the Great City, perhaps a name for the underworld.

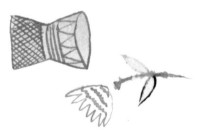